CARTWHEELS

Little Elephant's Moon

Adèle Geras

Illustrated by
Linda Birch

First published in Great Britain 1986
by Hamish Hamilton Children's Books
Garden House 57–59 Long Acre London WC2E 9JZ
Text copyright © 1986 by Adèle Geras
Illustrations copyright © 1986 by Linda Birch

For Susan and Gillian Eva

British Library Cataloguing in Publication Data
Geras, Adèle
Little elephant's moon.——Cartwheels
I. Title II. Birch, Linda III. Series
823'.914[J]   PZ7

ISBN 0–241–11729–1

Colour separations by Anglia Reproductions
Typeset by Katerprint Co. Ltd, Oxford
Printed in Great Britain by
Blantyre Printing and Binding Ltd
London and Glasgow

It was night-time in the jungle. All the animals had eaten their supper and were getting ready for bed.

As they were settling down to sleep,
Giraffe looked up into the sky. He saw the
moon shining brightly.

"I wish I could have the moon to keep,"
he said. "It would make a lovely hat. I
would call it my moonshine hat."

"I'd like to have the moon to keep, too,"
said Leopard. "It would make a nice
bright button for my coat."

Tiger looked up from his den.

"It would make a fine gold medal to
pin to my chest," he said.

Snake thought it was just the right size
for him to curl up in.

"A big, round bed," he said. "Fancy!"

"We think it looks like a pond," said
the birds and the butterflies. "We have
wings. Maybe we could fly up to the moon
and swim in it?"

Then Momma Elephant looked up into the sky. "I think the moon would make a beautiful dish," she said. "My mango pie would look so delicious on it."

Little Six opened her eyes, sleepily.
"Anyone can see it's a ball," she said.
"A lovely shining ball to play with. Will
you get it for me for my birthday, Momma?"

"But it's your birthday tomorrow!" said
Momma Elephant. "There isn't much
time to go and get it, but I'll try." And she
kissed her youngest baby good-night.

When all the little elephants were
asleep, she went across to Giraffe's house.

"Little Six wants the moon for her
birthday," she said. "Can you reach it
with your long neck?"

"No, I can't. I have tried many times. I
have even stood on a chair, but I can't
reach the moon," Giraffe said.

So Momma Elephant went over to
Tiger's den.

"Can you reach the moon, Tiger?" she
asked. "Little Six wants it for her
birthday."

But even when Tiger made his biggest leap, he couldn't reach the moon.

Momma Elephant was going to ask Snake, but she changed her mind.

"Snake has no head for heights. He's always sliding along the ground. He wouldn't even try to reach the moon."

So she went across to Leopard's tree.
Leopard was fast asleep.

"Excuse me," said Momma Elephant.

"What! Who goes there?" growled
Leopard. "Oh, it's you, Momma
Elephant, what's the matter?"

Momma Elephant told Leopard her
problem.

"I'm afraid that no one can reach the
moon," said Leopard. "It's far too high.
Even the birds and the butterflies can't
reach it. I am sorry."

"Oh dear," sighed Momma Elephant.
"Little Six will be so disappointed."
"Don't worry," said Leopard. "I have
an idea which may help you."

The next day, Momma Elephant iced the birthday cake and set out the dishes and cups for the party.

All the animals from near-by came to
celebrate Little Six's birthday.

They played games and sang songs.
And Little Six had so many wonderful
presents that she forgot about the moon.

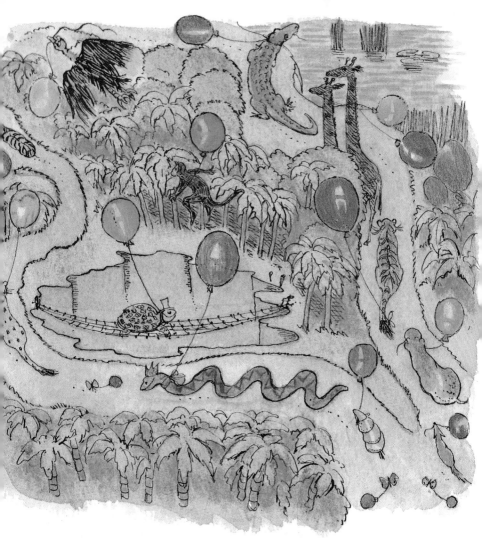

Slowly the sun went down and the sky
grew dark. It was almost night-time when
the animals went home. They were all full
of cake and orange squash and jellies and
crisps.

"Soon the moon will be up," Momma
Elephant said quietly, "and Little Six will
want it. I shall have to tell her that the
moon is too high up for anyone to reach it."

Suddenly Leopard came running
along. He was kicking something with his
paws. It was something large and round
and shiny.

"Sorry, I'm late!" he cried. "I have a
present for Little Six. It's a ball from –"
    Little Six did not let him finish what he
was saying. "It's the moon!" she cried.
"The moon to play with and kick around.
And it's mine!"

24

Little Six ran off with the shiny, yellow ball.

"Where did you find such a ball, Leopard?" asked Momma Elephant.

"I went to the school in the village. It was their Sports Day today. The people were so surprised to see me that they all ran away. But they left their ball behind. I knew Little Six would like it because it is bright and shiny, like the moon."

"You are a good friend," said Momma Elephant. "Thank you."

That night, when Little Six saw the
moon up in the sky, she said sleepily,

"Someone has put an ordinary ball up
there, now that I've got the moon. You
can see it's not as shiny as *my* moon."

"That's right, Little Six," said Momma
Elephant. "Now go to sleep, till the sun
comes up." And she kissed her smallest
child good-night and tiptoed away.